This book belongs to:

....

For Bader and Mira, who gave my life meaning and teach me everyday.
May our hair always be curly.
Maryam

For Mora Juncal, an extraordinary friend whose hair resembles Mira's:
wild and free.
Rebeca

First published in the United Kingdom in 2019 by Lantana Publishing Ltd., London.
www.lantanapublishing.com

American edition published in 2019 by Lantana Publishing Ltd., UK.
info@lantanapublishing.com

Text © Maryam al Serkal 2019
Illustration © Rebeca Luciani 2019

The moral rights of the author and illustrator have been asserted.

Distributed in the United States and Canada by Lerner Publishing Group, Inc.
241 First Avenue North, Minneapolis, MN 55401 U.S.A.
For reading levels and more information, look for this title at www.lernerbooks.com
Cataloging-in-Publication Data Available.

Printed and bound in Europe.
Original artwork created with acrylics on paper, completed digitally.

ISBN: 978-1-911373-61-2
eBook ISBN: 978-1-911373-64-3

Mira's Curly Hair

Maryam al Serkal

Rebeca Luciani

LANTANA
PUBLISHING

Mira had very **curly** hair. It **curled** at the front.
It **curled** at the back. It **curled** everywhere!

Mira didn't like her hair. She wanted it to be
STRAIGHT and **SMOOTH**,
just like her Mama's.

She tried to pull it down,
but it still *curled* up.

She stood on her head, but the **curling** wouldn't stop!

She used some old books to STRAIGHTEN out her hair...

...but when she got up,

there were *curls* everywhere!

Mira wanted her hair to be

STRAIGHT

and

SMOOTH

just like her Mama's.

One cloudy day, Mira went for a
stroll holding her Mama's hand.

Drip, drip, drip,

rain started to fall.

They ran towards
a palm areesh,

and crouched among
the chicks and geese.

As they sat waiting for the rain to clear, Mira looked at her Mama and started to stare…

Mama's hair was *curling*! Up and up!
It kept on *curling*! It wouldn't stop!

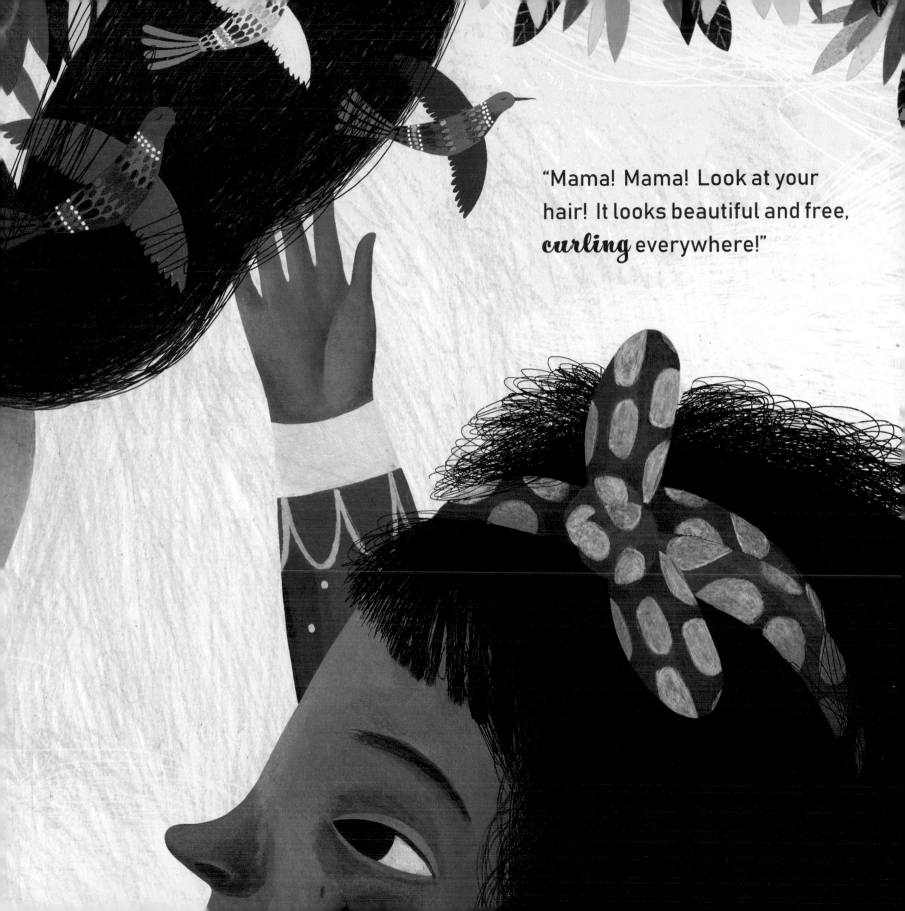

"Mama! Mama! Look at your hair! It looks beautiful and free, *curling* everywhere!"

From that day on, *curls* were the only way Mira and her Mama wore their hair every day.

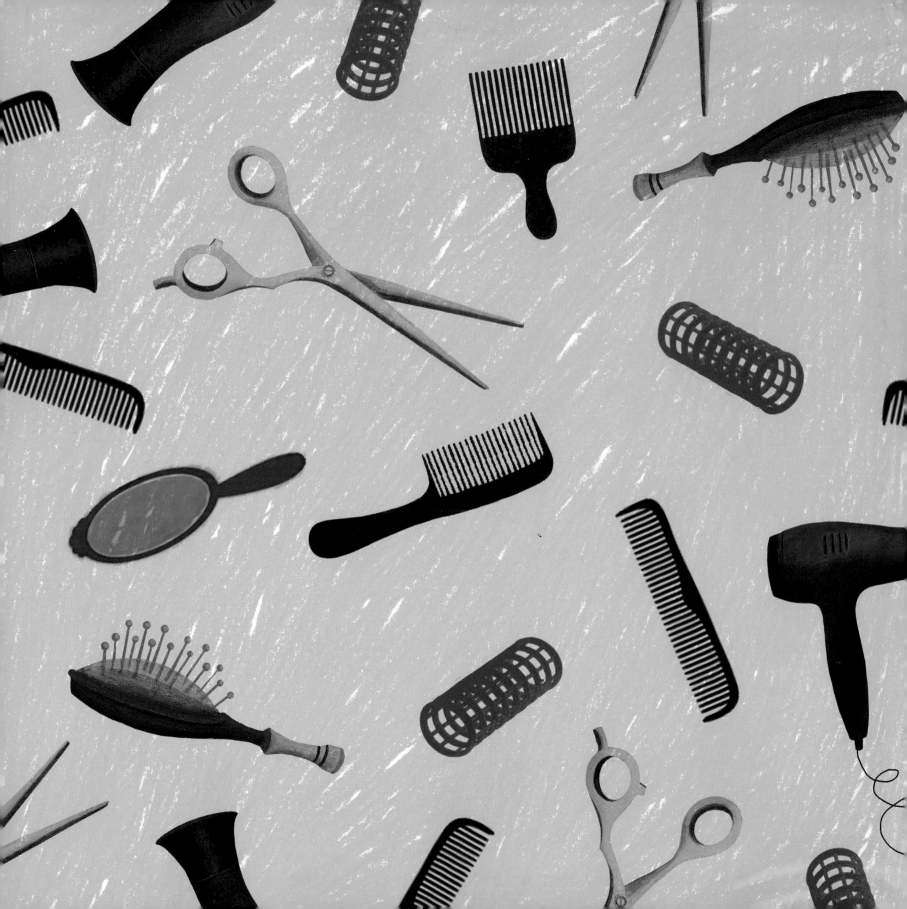